D1200166

Mila's
BIG EASY DAY

Written by: **JEAN ROUSSEAU LAWRENCE**   Illustrated by: **KELLEY CHAUVIN**

Mila's BIG EASY Day

Written by: Jean Rousseau Lawrence

Illustrated by: Kelley Chauvin

ISBN: 978-1-66786-081-7

© 2022. All rights reserved. No part of this publication may be reproduced, distributed, or transmitted in any form or by any means, including photocopying, recording, or other electronic or mechanical methods, without the prior written permission of the publisher, except in the case of brief quotations embodied in critical reviews and certain other noncommercial uses permitted by copyright law.

MILA'S BIG EASY DAY

Follow along with Mila Rose on this adventure as she takes her grandmas on a fun romp, traveling by streetcar, through the "Big Easy" City of New Orleans. As they ride down the streetcar line they meet different people and enjoy many stops along the way. They visit the zoo, the aquarium, and the cathedral. They eat snacks, lunch, listen to jazz music, and see boats on the river. These grandmas spill, get hungry, walk slowly, make messes and need naps, but they are very happy. As they all sit together at the last stop, Café du Monde, they celebrate their day with coffee and donuts. Mila then realizes that keeping up with two grandmas was fun but really isn't so easy after all!

This book is told through the eyes of a young girl. It can be read in its entirety by the older reader or you can choose to read a few of the titled adventures each day. The beautiful illustrations are each works of art and there are blank pages in the back for your little artist to enjoy coloring. There is also a picture of Mila for you to cut out, then take on your own adventure. Please upload pictures of yourself to Facebook at Mila's Big Easy Day, so we can learn about many other places too!

For Mila, Jackson, Isaac and Anna, who have filled my heart with so much love. You are each a special blessing for which I am eternally grateful.

ACKNOWLEDGMENTS:

A special thank you to my husband, Jim, who loves and supports me and all my hobbies (and there are many). Your constant support to me, our children and grandchildren is inspirational. You are our rock. I love you.

Stephanie, Jude, Chad, Amy, Julie and Linda....thanks for your constant love and support. You all mean everything to me.

And most importantly thanks to God, who leads my path and shines His light along the way.
PSALM 23

ADDITIONAL THANKS TO:

Artist/Illustrator, Kelley Chauvin for beautifully bringing my ideas to life.

Mila,
You are the author of your life's story. May it be filled with safe adventure, much love, and lots of laughter.
Love always, Queenie

STORIES

SIGHT WORDS

Each paragraph throughout the story has a word or two in all caps from the word bank below. This will allow your child to join in as you read, and learn some sight words along the way.

MAP

GREEN

HAPPY

ZOO

GIRAFFE

MONKEY

LION

TIGER

PINK

RED

YELLOW

WHITE

HOT DOG

CLARINET

SHARK

CHURCH

COFFEE

DONUTS

BIG EASY DAY

Hello! My name is Mila Rose. In my family I have two grandmas, one is named Queenie and the other is named Nana. They've been really good lately, so I thought it would be nice to take them on a fun adventure.

They were excited when I told them we would be riding the famous streetcars through the "BIG EASY" City of New Orleans! My Mom gave me a MAP so I'd know where to go.

THE STREETCAR

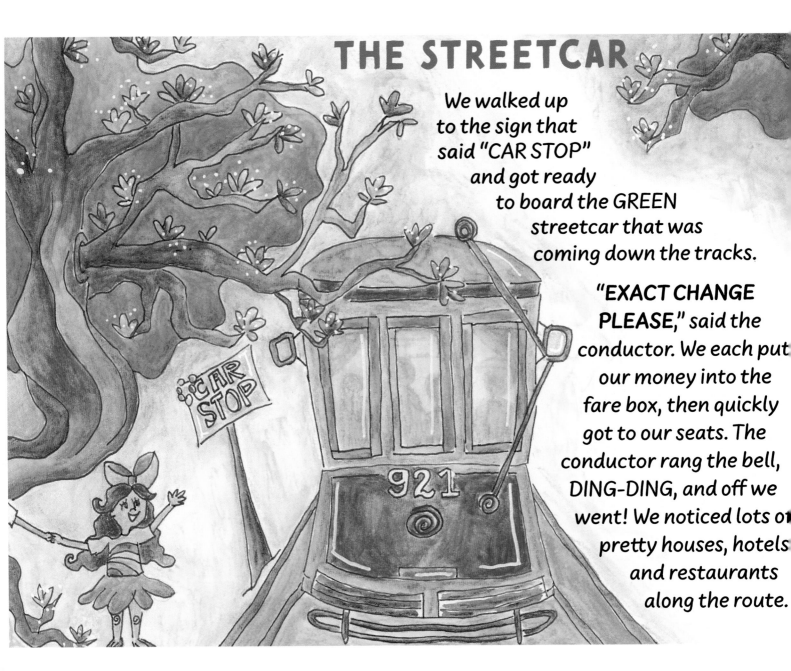

We walked up to the sign that said "CAR STOP" and got ready to board the GREEN streetcar that was coming down the tracks.

"**EXACT CHANGE PLEASE**," said the conductor. We each put our money into the fare box, then quickly got to our seats. The conductor rang the bell, DING-DING, and off we went! We noticed lots of pretty houses, hotels and restaurants along the route.

Some of the people riding along with us were dressed in different types of clothes. I wondered, where are all these people going? One lady on the streetcar was wearing a green shirt, YELLOW shorts, and a safari hat!

THE ZOOKEEPER

I said to the lady wearing the safari hat, "Good morning, I'm Mila. I'm taking my grandmas on an adventure. Where are you going today?"

She smiled and said, "I'm going to work. I am a zookeeper at Audubon Zoo. I help take care of all the animals who live there. Maybe you could take your grandmas to the ZOO today!" Nana and Queenie love animals, so I thought the ZOO was a great idea.

When the conductor stopped the streetcar she said, "AUDUBON ZOO," so we all got off and walked to the entrance. The zookeeper smiled, waved and said "Have fun with your grandmas today!" Just then a giant colorful bird called a macaw flew up to greet her!

As we walked into the zoo we saw a big elephant. It was a fountain that had water squirting out of it's trunk. There were also pretty flamingos and some seals that were making a barking sound!

THE ZOO

I took Queenie and Nana to see the GIRAFFE first. I reminded them not to get too close to the animals. Queenie was wearing a sun hat with big PINK flowers on top. She was saying, "Good morning GIRAFFE," when all of a sudden he stuck his very long neck over the fence and snatched her hat!

"Ah, my hat!" Squealed Queenie. Well.....the GIRAFFE seemed to really like those PINK flowers and ate one! He then chewed the hat and spit it out! Queenie laughed, ran over, picked up her chewed hat and put it back on her head. What a silly GIRAFFE!

After the hat incident we walked through the zoo to see the other animals. We saw a LION, a TIGER, and some cute little turtles playing on a tree branch. The bees were bumbling and the butterflies were fluttering.

SNOWBALLS

When we left the zoo we thought an icy cold snowball would be the perfect treat. The snowball stand was just a short ride on the streetcar. There were so many flavors that it was hard for me to choose, so I picked a rainbow which is many colors and flavors on one snowball!

Nana ordered a RED cherry flavor and Queenie chose a YELLOW ice cream flavored snowball.

As we sat on a bench and ate our snowballs I heard Nana say, "Oopsies," and I noticed she had spilled some of her RED snowball on one of her new WHITE shoes.

Nana tried to wipe her shoe but it didn't come off. Now she had a big RED stain on her WHITE shoe. I told her, "That's ok Nana....sometimes grandmas spill too!"

Queenie was wearing her chewed up hat and Nana had a RED stain on her shoe, but it didn't matter because my grandmas seemed really HAPPY!

BAKER MAN

Another streetcar was coming, so we hopped back on and headed down the line. This time we sat next to a man with a big WHITE hat. I said, "Hi, I'm Mila, and I'm on an adventure with my grandmas. Are you a painter?"

The man said, "No, I'm a pastry chef, but some people call me 'The Baker Man.' I make all the fancy desserts at a very busy bakery. I make lots of cakes, cookies, and pies. I hope you come to try one of my desserts.

When you do, I'll make you and your grandmas a cake with extra sprinkles!" Then he handed me a card with his name on it. It said:

JACKSON
Pastry Chef
PHILLIPS

The streetcar stopped and the pastry chef got off. He waved as he walked into the bakery. I closed my eyes and tried to imagine all the beautiful cakes and treats he would make that day. I think it would be hard to chose just one!

HOT DOG TIME

As we rode along my grandmas started saying, "We want a snack. We're hungry." So I thought it was time to feed my grandmas lunch. I really didn't want to have hungry, grumpy grandmas!

A man sitting across from us was wearing a RED and WHITE shirt. On his head was a **crazy** hat with a big HOT DOG on top! The conductor stopped the streetcar, rang the bell, then said loudly, "AQUARIUM, HAPPY DOGS." The man with the crazy HOT DOG hat stood up and said, "That's me!"

I told my grandmas, "Hey, he must be the HOT DOG man! Come on…..let's go!" The HOT DOG man got off really fast, but my grandmas move kind of slow. I said, "Come on Queenie. Come on Nana…you can do it!" We got off the streetcar and followed the man with the crazy hat. We went as fast as grandma feet would go…and just so you know, grandma feet don't move too fast!

We followed the man to a cart that looked like a **giant** HOT DOG. It said, "HAPPY DOGS" on the side. Queenie and Nana started saying, "HOT-DOG, HOT-DOG, HOT- DOG!" I reminded them that they should always ask nicely.

I ordered 3 HOT DOGS. I just wanted ketchup on mine.
Nana wanted mustard and ketchup, and Queenie wanted chili.
We all took a bite and thought they tasted really yummy!

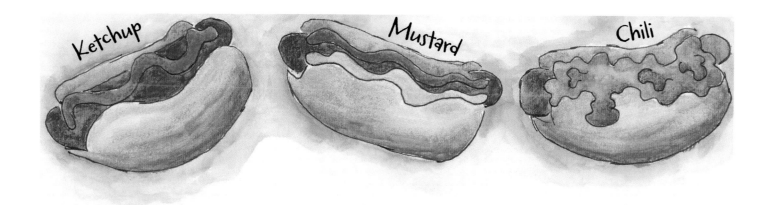

JAZZY MUSIC

While we were eating our HOT DOGS we heard some very jazzy music. We turned around and through the crowd we actually saw the lady who was playing that jazzy music!

Queenie said her name is **Doreen Ketchens** and she was playing an instrument called a CLARINET. I couldn't believe it, but she was actually playing with her eyes closed!

The sound of the music coming out of the CLARINET was amazing and I noticed that everyone was smiling as they listened.

My grandmas seemed to **really** like that jazzy music and they started dancing! Yes.....it's true, dancing grandmas! And while they were dancing they both spilled their HOT DOGS on their shirts. Now they had big stains on their shirts, a chewed hat, and a RED stained shoe, but they didn't mind at all. They were HAPPY! Queenie said, "Well Mila, sometimes grandmas are a little messy." They laughed, then they kept on dancing!

THE AQUARIUM

After my grandmas finished all that dancing, we walked over to the Aquarium to look at the sea animals. The first thing we saw was a giant glass tunnel that we walked under to watch all the marine life. I learned that marine life is all the things that live in the ocean, including plants. I didn't even know that plants could live under water!

The giant tank was full of colorful fish and underwater plants. There was even a SHARK with **very** pointy teeth that made my grandmas a little scared. I told them not to worry because the sea animals cannot get through the big arched glass.

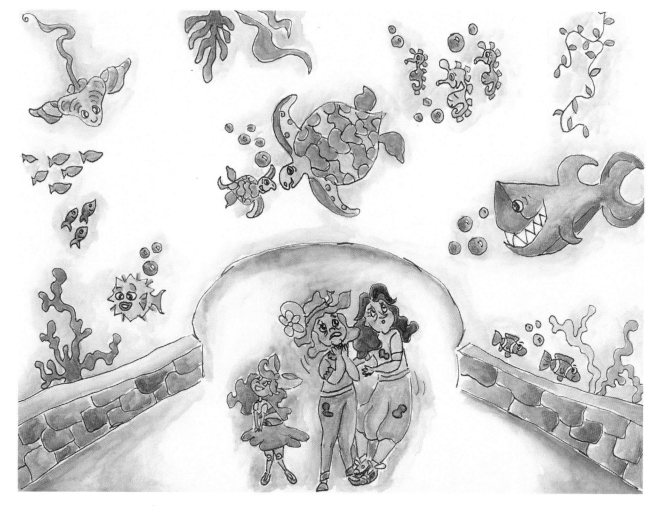

I loved watching the sea turtles and the blow fish.

Queenie and Nana would jump, and squeal, and laugh, every time the SHARK swam by. It made me giggle to see my grandmas having so much fun!

CHURCH

My grandmas were getting a little tired, but they wanted to go to a CHURCH to light a candle and pray. I looked on the MAP my mom gave me and I saw that a big, fancy CHURCH called St. Louis Cathedral was a short streetcar ride away.

We boarded a RED streetcar for the last ride of the day. We could see the Mississippi River on one side and a giant CHURCH steeple on the other side. There was even a boat going by on the river that was playing music. Nana said that the music was from an instrument called a calliope (ka-LIE-ah-pee).

I helped my grandmas off the streetcar and we walked into the
St. Louis Cathedral. My grandmas kept **talking** and **talking** about
how beautiful the cathedral was inside. I reminded them they
should whisper if they have to talk in CHURCH. They both smiled,
lit a candle, bowed their heads, then quietly said a prayer.

COFFEE AND DONUTS

Now Queenie and Nana were **very** tired and **really** needed a nap, but I had one more surprise for them today. Across the street from the cathedral was Cafe du Monde, a famous DONUT stand.

They make the best DONUTS called beignets, (you say it like bin-yays) and the best COFFEE called Cafe au Lait (cafe-o-lay). Queenie said those are French words.

My grandmas love coffee so I thought this would be a great way to end our adventure. We sat at a table and ordered 3 DONUTS, 2 cups of COFFEE, and a chocolate milk for me.

The little square DONUTS had a lot of powdered sugar on top that flew into the air and onto us as we ate them. It made us laugh to see that we all had white sugar on our clothes.

We smiled, then held up our drinks and said, **"CHEERS!"**

TIME TO GO HOME

Queenie and Nana both gave me a tight hug and thanked me for such a fun day. They looked really messy with the chewed hat, stained shoe, HOT DOG spills, and WHITE powdered sugar on their shirts, but there were so HAPPY! I felt really HAPPY too, but I've realized that grandmas aren't so easy after all. I've learned that grandmas are VERY... HARD... WORK!

As we rode home Queenie and Nana both fell sound asleep……….SHHHHHHHHH…….my grandmas are sleeping.

THE END

COLOR THEN ASK AN ADULT TO CUT OUT THE PICTURE
SO YOU CAN TAKE MILA ON SOME OF YOUR ADVENTURES.
WITH ADULT PERMISSION, POST YOUR PICTURES TO
"MILA'S BIG EASY DAY" ON FACEBOOK. THEN WE CAN ALL
LEARN ABOUT OTHER PLACES TOO!

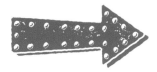

ABOUT THE AUTHOR:

Jean Rousseau Lawrence was born in New Orleans and was raised in a nearby suburb where she and her family enjoyed the many activities and culture of the city. Her love for riding streetcars began after she attended a birthday party on a decorated streetcar that rode up and down St. Charles Ave.

She is a wife, mother, and grandmother who believes her biggest treasure is her family and any time spent with family and friends. After retiring from a career as a Registered Nurse, she now has time to further pursue hobbies and enjoys photography, cooking, music, watercolors, pottery and now writing. She currently has plans for 3 additional books that will feature Imaginative Isaac, Adorable Anna, and a Mardi Gras Parade in honor of her mothers love of parades.

For book signings and general information contact Jean at:
MilasBigEasyDay@gmail.com or Milas Big Easy Day on Facebook

ABOUT THE ILLUSTRATOR:

Kelley Chauvin was raised in a suburb of New Orleans. She received a Bachelors of Art from LSU. She has always had a love for drawing, painting, musical arts, make up artistry, and roller skating. These hobbies fill her spare time and she still loves to roller skate! To contact the Kelley for art projects or commission work email: kel@pinkcloudart.com

ABOUT MILA:

Mila Rose is a sweet little girl who loves her family, her pets, butterflies, rainbows, unicorns, dancing and playing with Barbie's and Lego's. She frequently enjoys time and adventures with her Queenie and Nana.

TO ORDER BOOKS GO TO: STORE.BOOKBABY.COM, BOOKBABY.COM AND CHOOSE "BOOKSHOP" FROM THE DROP DOWN, BARNES AND NOBLE, AMAZON, OR FOR BULK ORDERS CONTACT YOUR BOOK SUPPLIER.